THE CUCKOO BIRD

The Cuckoo Bird
Text copyright © 1988 by Judy Corbalis
Illustrations copyright © 1988 by David Armitage
First published by André Deutsch Limited, 105-106 Great Russell Street, London WC1B 3LJ
Printed in the U.S.A. All rights reserved.
1 2 3 4 5 6 7 8 9 10
First American Edition, 1991

Library of Congress Cataloging-in-Publication Data
Corbalis, Judy.
  The cuckoo bird / by Judy Corbalis ; illustrated by David
Armitage.
      p.   cm.
  Summary: A little girl and her grandmother try to outwit a shape-
changing, greedy cuckoo bird who has tricked his way into their
house.
  ISBN 0-06-021697-2. — ISBN 0-06-021698-0 (lib. bdg.)
  [1. Cuckoos—Fiction.   2. Behavior—Fiction.]   I. Armitage,
David, date, ill. II. Title.
PZ7.C798Cu 1991   90-22576
[E]—dc20   CIP
                                                                AC

THE CUCKOO BIRD

by Judy Corbalis
illustrated by David Armitage

HarperCollins*Publishers*

The Cuckoo Bird came
to the little girl's door.

Knock! Knock!

"Who's there?"
cried the little girl.

"A handsome soldier!"
called the Cuckoo Bird.
"Let me in!"

"I can't," said the little girl.
"My grandmother told
me not to. She says
the Cuckoo Bird is about."

"You can see I'm no bird.
I'm a soldier. I'm hungry,
little girl. Let me in."

"No!" said the little girl, opening the door and peeping through the crack. "I'm too busy. I'm sweeping."

"Let me in," begged the soldier. "I'll help you. I'm good with a broom."

"So am I," said the little girl. "Now be off with you!" And she shut the door tight.

Away went the Cuckoo Bird-soldier across the hill. He blew on his magic pipes and changed into an old, old man.

Back over the hill he crept and shuffled up to the little girl's door.
Tap! Tap!
"Who's there?" cried the little girl.
"A poor old man. Help me," he sighed.

Out to the doorstep she came.
   "What can I do for you, poor old man?"

"Let me in, little girl, and make me a cup of tea, for pity's sake."
   "Oh, sir," said the little girl. "I'll make you a cup of tea with pleasure, but let you in I cannot. I promised my grandmother."

"I want to drink it inside," said the old man crossly. "Let me in at once."
   "I told you I can't," said the little girl, "so you can just go without your tea."
   And she shut the door tight in his face.

Over the hill went the old man-Cuckoo Bird. He blew on his magic pipes. Bit by bit, he changed into a baby.

"This will be a slow journey," he said to himself, as he crawled back over the hill to the little girl's door.

Scratch! Scratch!
"Who's there?" cried the little girl.
But the Cuckoo Bird-baby only gurgled.

The little girl came out to the step. "Oh look!" she said. "It's a baby."
"Someone must have left him there," she thought. "Grandmother told
me not to let anyone in, but I can't leave a baby outside on its own."

She laid him in the cradle
by the hearth and tucked
a shawl around him.
    "Pretty boy," she said.

"Feed me!" cried the
Cuckoo-baby. "I'm starving!"

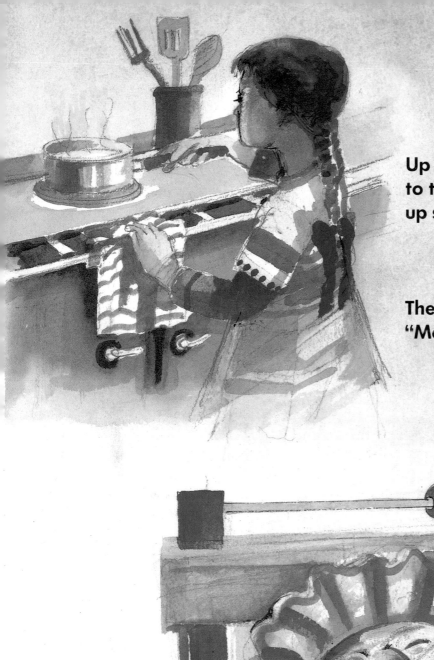

Up jumped the little girl. She ran to the stove and warmed up some milk for him.

Guzzle, guzzle.

The Cuckoo-baby swallowed it all. "More! More!" hc shouted.

The little girl ran to the cookie jar
and gave him a handful of gingersnaps.
Crunch, crunch, crunch, crunch.
The Cuckoo-baby gobbled them
all up.

"Food! Food!" he screamed.
The little girl looked at him.
"He's growing," she said,
aghast.
The Cuckoo-baby climbed
out of the cradle and pulled up
a stool to the table.

He banged very hard with his spoon.
"I want more! I want more!"

The little girl cooked him an egg
and sardines, some biscuits
and potatoes and cupcakes.

But still he was hungry.
  "There's only the chicken," she cried
in despair. "And that's for Sunday.
What can I do?"
  She cooked up the chicken.

But still he was hungry.
  "Now there's no more food
in the house," wept the little girl.

The Cuckoo-baby had grown very fast.
He popped out of his suit.
"Give me some clothes!" he demanded,
and he put on the little girl's jacket.

"Give me your paints and your dolls' house! Give me your train set! Give me your thimble!"

"No!" cried the little girl. "I've given you enough. You can't take everything. Stop it at once!"

"It's *not* enough! I want more!!!" roared the Cuckoo-baby.

"You're greedy," said the little girl. "Don't be so selfish."

"You're rude!" shouted the Cuckoo-baby. And he broke the arm off her doll. "You let me in. Now you must look after me."

"I want you to go home," sobbed the little girl.

"I live here now," said the Cuckoo-baby. "Give me your bed. I'm tired." And he climbed into the little girl's bed and was asleep in two minutes.

The little girl lay on the floor by the fire and tried to sleep, but she was crying.

Just then the door opened and her grandmother came in.

"Whatever are you doing out here on the floor?" she asked.

"Oh, Grandmother," wept the little girl. "A soldier came and I sent him away. Then an old man tapped at the door and I kept him out, too. But there was a baby, only a little one, lying on the doorstep, so I carried him into the house . . ."

"And then you had nothing but trouble," said her grandmother grimly. "That's no ordinary infant, I'll be bound."

And she slipped into the little girl's room to have a look at him.

"Just as I thought," she said. "It's a Cuckoo-baby. The very worst sort. We'll have to get rid of him."

"But he said he lives here now," said the little girl.

"Just a minute," said her grandmother. "I'm thinking. . . . I remember my grandmother telling me when I was a little girl how she once let the Cuckoo Bird inside the house."

"Did she get rid of him?" asked the little girl.

"Yes," said her grandmother, frowning, "but I can't remember how. I know she hit him with the broom but that didn't work, and she . . ."

"Try and remember. Please," begged the little girl.

"I'm trying," said the old lady. And she closed her eyes so she could think better.

The little girl waited a minute. And another. And another. She peeped at her grandmother, but the old lady didn't stir.

She shook her grandmother gently and whispered in her ear, "Grandmother! You're not paying attention to me."

The old lady opened her eyes and sat up straight.

"No attention! That's it! I've remembered. That's what she did! She paid no attention to him! Quick! We have to hurry."

Very quietly, they slipped outside and hid behind the currant bushes. "We must stay here till the sun comes up, then watch through the window and not say a word," said the grandmother. The little girl snuggled against her.

Dawn broke.

Inside the house, the Cuckoo-baby woke up. He screamed for his breakfast, but nobody came.

The little girl and her grandmother watched silently.

The Cuckoo-baby grew angry. He ranted and roared. But the little girl and her grandmother still didn't make a sound.

The Cuckoo-baby flew into a fit of temper and hurled the furniture all around the room. The little girl and her grandmother never stirred.

"How *dare* he behave like that?" thought the little girl. Suddenly, she had an idea.

"Move closer to the door," she whispered to her grandmother, "and as soon as he comes out, run inside as fast as you can."

"Whatever are you going to do?" asked her grandmother.
    "I haven't got time to explain," said the little girl. "Just do as I say."
    And she crept noiselessly to the back of the yard and hid behind the apple tree.

"I've got a lovely apple here," she shouted at the top of her voice, "and *you're* not getting it."

The Cuckoo-baby gave a scream of rage and burst out of the house. Quickly, the grandmother darted in through the door behind him. The little girl threw the apple as hard as she could at the fence. The Cuckoo-baby flapped furiously toward it.

"I'll get you, you wicked girl!" he screamed. "Give that to me. I should have it. Everything's for me."

"No it's not!!" cried the little girl as she raced toward the house. "You're nothing but a stupid, greedy bird. You'll never get back into our house again."

And she sped in through the door and slammed the bolt behind her.

"Clever girl," said her grandmother, hugging her tight.

"I'm sorry I let him in," said the little girl.

"Never mind," said her grandmother. "Many an older and wiser person than you has been tricked by the Cuckoo Bird. But he's eaten all the chicken, so we'll have to have onion soup for supper."

"I like onion soup," said the little girl. "And I promise I'll never let *anyone* strange in the house again."

And she never did.

Over the hill, the Cuckoo Bird settled his ruffled feathers and gobbled up a juicy earthworm.

"I'm a Cuckoo Bird," he sang with his mouth full. "I'm a Cuckoo Bird. Not many people get the better of me."

And he pulled out his magic pipes and played himself a comforting little tune.